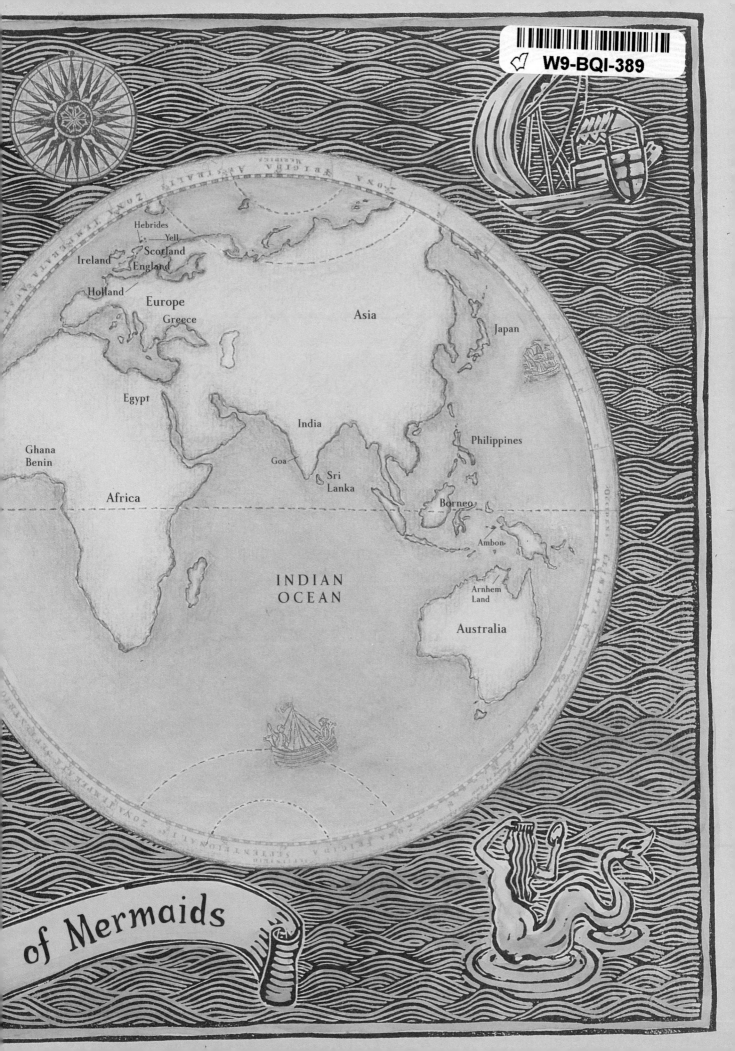

of Mermaids

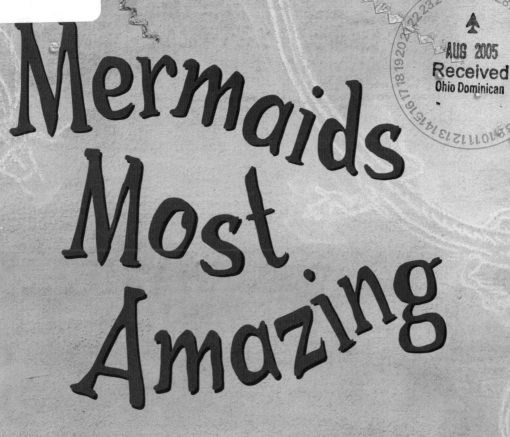

Mermaids Most Amazing

Written and illustrated by

NARELLE OLIVER

G. P. PUTNAM'S SONS · NEW YORK

For Jess, Liam, and Tashi

First American Edition published in 2005 by G. P. Putnam's Sons, a division of Penguin Young Readers Group,

345 Hudson Street, New York, NY 10014. G. P. Putnam's Sons, Reg. U.S. Pat. & Tm. Off.

First published by Omnibus Books, a division of Scholastic Australia Pty Limited, in 2001.

This edition published under license from Scholastic Australia Pty Limited.

Printed in Singapore by Tien Wah Press (Pte) Ltd.

Designed by Marikka Tamura. Text set in Indispose Medium.

Narelle Oliver used hand-colored linocuts and collage for the illustrations for this book.

Library of Congress Cataloging-in-Publication Data

Oliver, Narelle, 1960–

Mermaids most amazing / written and illustrated by Narelle Oliver. — 1st American ed.   p. cm.

Includes bibliographical references.

1. Mermaids. I. Title.

GR910.O55 2005   398.21—dc22   2004001889

ISBN 0-399-24288-0

1 3 5 7 9 10 8 6 4 2

First American Edition

This project has been assisted by the Commonwealth Government through the Australia Council,

its arts funding and advisory body; and Arts Queensland through

the Arts and Museums Development Programs of Assistance.

Contents

Real, Unreal, or Just a Seal?

For as long as anyone can remember, mermaids have swum through our stories and splashed through our dreams.

Where did they come from? Could it be that real mermaids did exist, once upon a time?

Some say that mermaids are simply creatures of make-believe from long ago. Ancient legends tell of fishtailed gods and powerful water spirits. Perhaps these were the first mermaids.

The Polynesian god Vatea was the legendary creator of the islands Tahiti and Hawaii.

In Hindu mythology, the god Vishnu became half fish to warn people that huge floods were coming.

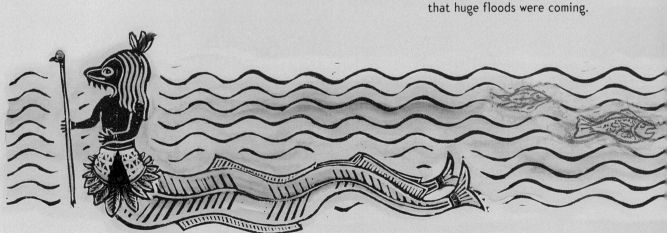

Facing Page: The Babylonian god Oannes (5000 B.C.)

A man-fish with a porpoise face and two tails led ancestors of the Native American Shawano people across the "Great Salt Lake" from Asia to North America.

Since those early times, mermaids have appeared in folktales and myths in almost every corner of the world.

There are mermaids in the sea, mermaids in lakes, mermaids in rivers, ponds, and wells.

Even in deserts far from the sea, there are mermaids.

Scottish fairy folk called Selkies are able to live underwater by wearing magic sealskins.

An evil blood-drinking mermaid lives in a Scottish lake.

In a Filipino folktale, a child is secretly changed into a mermaid by the fish king.

Ukrainian mermaids sing before storms at sea.

Maraki-hau, the ocean gods of the New Zealand Maoris, have long tongues for sucking up fish.

This Japanese mermaid, or *ningyo*, is carved onto a small wooden purse called a *netsuke*.

In Mexican folklore, a mermaid lives in an oasis in the Sonoran Desert.

Some medieval English mermaids have bird features.

In Ghana, a powerful mermaid called Tahbi-yin lives in a rock. People believe she can cause drowning.

A magic cap allows Irish mermaids and mermen, called *merrows,* to live below the sea.

Merrows sometimes change into little hornless cows.

In Europe, webbed fingers may be the sign of a mermaid's child.

For the Rembarrnga people, long waterweeds are the hair of Yawkyawk the mermaid spirit.

The German *nix,* or water elf, can have a fish tail and green teeth.

In the legends of the Rembarrnga Aboriginal people of Arnhem Land, Australia, the roar of a waterfall is the voice of a mermaid spirit named Yawkyawk.

Fifteenth-century European artists drew mermaids with different kinds of tails.

7

Long ago, sailors voyaged to exotic countries in search of gold or spices. Often they came home with tales of fabulous sea creatures. Perhaps they caught sight of mysterious sea mammals like the dugong, and that was how the stories of mermaids began.

Dugongs and their cousins the manatees are shy, secretive animals. They glide silently through swirling seagrass in warm, shallow seas, and sometimes in lakes and rivers. And they can behave in curiously human ways.

Seals, too, can look a little like people. Not so long ago, an unusual female seal was found near the islands of the Hebrides, off the coast of Scotland. The gray of its upper body had changed to pink. Seals like this may have been mistaken for mermaids throughout the ages.

Some reports suggest that the female manatee and dugong hold and feed their babies just as human mothers do.

Perhaps the mermaid is something more than a half-glimpsed sea mammal or ancient myth.

Many scientists say that life on Earth began in the water. Over millions of years, various water-dwelling animals grew legs, developed stronger lungs and skeletons, and moved onto the land.

Who knows what strange relatives these creatures left behind in the sea?

"And on Friday, the fourth of January in the year 1493, we saw three Mermaids leaping a good height out of the Sea, creatures not so faire as they are painted, somewhat resembling men in the face."
—Christopher Columbus

9

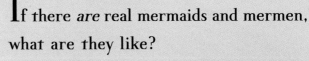

If there *are* real mermaids and mermen, what are they like?

From as early as A.D. 77, people wrote about mermaid sightings. Occasionally a live mermaid was captured, studied closely, and described in history and science books. If she was not returned to the sea, she never survived for long.

The most famous captive was the mermaid of Amboina. This little eel-shaped mermaid was caught off the coast of Borneo in Southeast Asia in 1712, and presented to the Dutch governor of Amboina province (now called Ambon) in Indonesia. She is supposed to have lived in a jar of water for four days and seven hours. During that time, she made sounds like a mouse and refused to eat.

Edam, Holland, 1403: During a violent storm, a mermaid floated through a broken dyke and was stranded in the mud.

New Orleans, Louisiana, 1881: The capture of a mermaid with claws was reported in a Boston newspaper.

Tanagra, Greece, A.D. 177: The Greek traveler and geographer Pausanias described a merman with gills and a dolphin tail, preserved in honey.

Benbecula, Hebrides, 1830: A boy threw a stone at a little sea-maiden playing in the waves. Her body was later washed ashore and given a proper funeral and burial.

River Nile, Egypt, A.D. 592: A "Sea-Man" and his female friend were observed for two hours as they swam in the river.

Many years ago, people believed that for every land animal, there was a similar animal in the sea. Horses, cows, and snakes existed on land, and, as everyone knew, there were sea horses, sea cows, and sea snakes.

Men and women lived on the land, so there must also be mermen and mermaids.

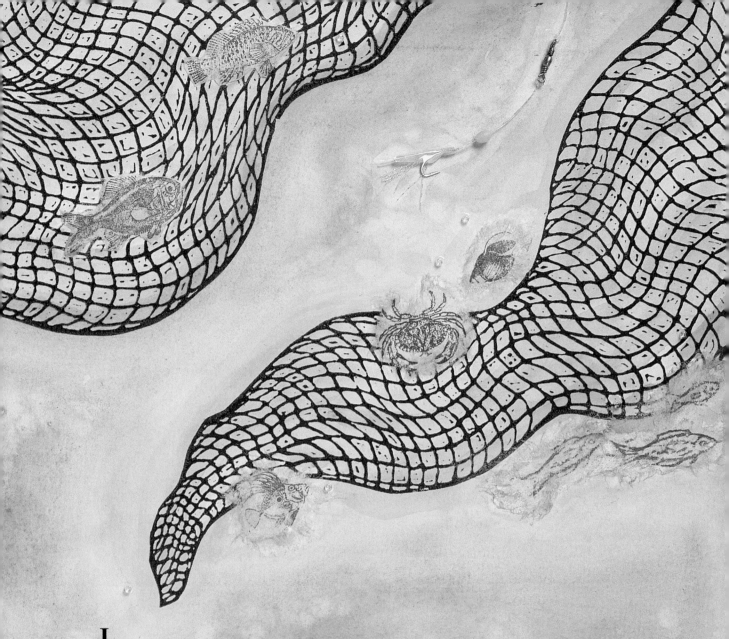

In 1833, six fishermen fishing off the Scottish Island of Yell hauled a strange mermaid into their boat. Her appearance was recorded in detail in a book called *The History of Whales and Seals.* She was about one meter long, and her body ended in a dogfish tail. Her face and neck were like a monkey's, and her head was covered in bristles that could stand up straight and then lie down flat like a cockatoo's crest.

The creature had no gills, fins, or webbed fingers, nor did she have scales or hair on her body. She did not struggle or bite, but lay in the boat with her arms folded, moaning softly.

The fishermen watched her closely for three hours. Finally, afraid she might die, they put her back in the water.

In an instant, the mermaid dived straight down out of sight.

From time to time, mermaids were washed ashore, and died there.

In 1560, some Jesuit priests claimed they had discovered seven mermaids and mermen beached on a tiny island west of Ceylon (now Sri Lanka). The bodies were taken to Goa in India, where a doctor cut them open to examine their internal organs. He declared that they were exactly the same as those of human beings.

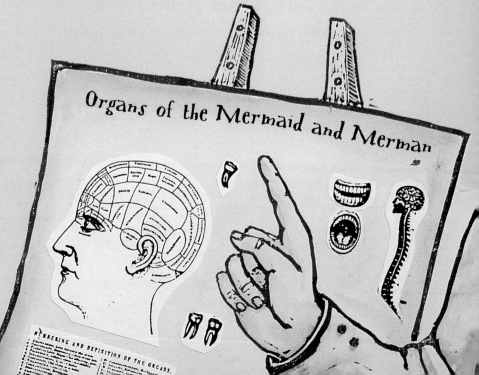

It would have been difficult to cut open and examine the gigantic mermaid found in A.D. 887 in Scotland, or Alba, as it was called then. According to a very old Irish history book, *The Annals of Ulster,* she was 195 feet long, her hair was eighteen feet long, and her nose and fingers measured seven feet. This means that the mermaid of Alba was as long as thirteen large cars placed end-to-end, and her fingers and nose were the length of a bed. She was also "whiter than the swan all over."

Organs of the Mermaid and Merman

Fakes and Frauds, Tricks and Treachery

Everybody wants to see a real mermaid or merman, but a good fake can be the next best thing. Throughout history, for all sorts of reasons, there has been some serious and not-so-serious trickery.

In the fourteenth century, King Chen of the small African country of Benin noticed that his legs were gradually becoming paralyzed. Fearful that he might be replaced by a healthier ruler, the king declared that he was changing into Olokun, god of sea and water, and his legs were transforming into mudfish. The people believed his story and never expected him to walk again. King Chen also insisted that his mudfish legs were sacred and should not be seen by others—so while he lived, his secret was never discovered.

Just for fun, an English vicar tricked crowds of villagers in 1826. One moonlit evening he swam out to a rock in the sea near the coastal town of Bude in Cornwall. He wrapped his legs in oilskins, put on a seaweed wig, and began to sing. Night after night he repeated his performance, and the local people flocked to watch.

Eventually the vicar grew tired of his practical joke—and his voice was hoarse. He sang "God Save the King," dived beneath the waves, and swam ashore. The mermaid of Bude was never seen again.

Being a fake was not so funny for a deformed man shipwrecked on an island in the late sixteenth century. Half starved, he was rescued by Spanish sailors who took him back to the mainland. His rescuers then placed him naked in a tub of water, gave him tattoos and makeup, and exhibited him for many days as a merman.

Fake mermaids and mermen have not always been live specimens.

In the early 1800s, it was not unusual to find shriveled little mermaid bodies on show in coffeehouses, taverns, and museums in cities like London and New York. These mermaids were usually made by joining the upper part of an orangutan to the tail end of a salmon. Japanese fishermen were especially skilled at making them, and some were very convincing.

One such mermaid was bought by a British seaman, Captain Eades, on a trip to the East Indies in 1822. He was convinced that the creature was real, and sold his ship in order to buy it. Before putting his mermaid on public display in London, he invited a respected scientist to examine it. As soon as the delicate silk wrappings were removed, the scientist declared the mermaid to be a fake made from parts of an orangutan, a baboon, and a salmon, with artificial fingernails and eyes.

This did not worry Captain Eades, nor did comments in the newspaper describing the creature as "a disgusting looking frightful monster." He exhibited his mermaid at the London Turf Club, where thousands of inquisitive visitors paid one shilling each to see it.

Fishtail Folktales

No matter where you go, mermaid magic is never far away.

In northern Australia, the mermaid spirit Yawkyawk has special powers for the Rembarrnga Aboriginal people. The legend of Yawkyawk (which the Rembarrnga call a "Dreaming") is told here by Bob Burruwal and Lena Yarinkura, who live in Bolkdjam, a remote place in north central Arnhem Land, Australia.

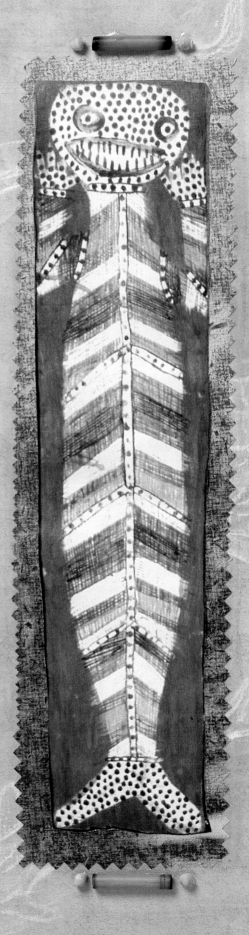

Yawkyawk Mermaid Dreaming

The Yawkyawk mermaid Dreaming lies there in the water for me. Long ago, Yawkyawk—the mermaid spirit—soaked herself in the river near Bolkdjam. She's the one who created the billabongs. She made the billabong near Bolkdjam.

"Sometimes, the Rainbow Serpent called Bolung and the mermaid called Yawkyawk are one and the same spirit. Yawkyawk and Bolung came up through the water and out of the ground. That spirit created the water and put it everywhere. Then she ate anything that was good, drowning it. After she had done that, everything grew up . . . all the fish, turtles, buffalo, all those things; . . . that short-necked turtle and the water goanna and all those water beetles, flat beetles, ducks, and all kinds of water animals . . . the stingray, long tom, saratoga, and barramundi."

("Billabongs" are small ponds near rivers. "Water goanna" are large Australian lizards.)

21

The Merman of Coos Bay

Long ago, a young Native American girl lived with her five brothers in Coos Bay on the North American Pacific coast. The girl was old enough to marry but preferred to be alone, exploring and swimming near their village.

One day, as she was returning from her swim, a strange man appeared before her.

"My village is at the bottom of the sea," he said. "Will you come with me and be my wife?"

"I cannot," the girl replied, "for if I go with you, I will never see my brothers again."

The merman promised that she could return to visit her brothers, and the girl agreed to become his wife.

She clung on to his belt, and down, down, down they went to the seabed, where many Indians lived in an underwater village. The merman was one of five sons of their chief.

The girl and the merman had a baby boy. When he was old enough, his mother made bows and arrows for him and taught him to hunt, telling him about his five uncles on the land and their fine bows and arrows. Soon the boy begged his father to let him meet his uncles.

The merman refused, but agreed that his wife might visit her brothers. The girl put on five otter skins and swam to the shore. Mistaking her for a real otter, the brothers shot arrows at her until her eldest brother recognized his lost sister.

The girl traded the otter skins for as many bows and arrows as she could carry. As she left, she told her brothers that they would find a whale on the beach the following day. The brothers did find a whale, and they shared the meat with all the people of the village.

That was the last time the girl visited her own people, but for many years afterward a whale was put ashore in summer and winter as a gift from the people of the sea.

The Sea~Maid and the Apsara

Many years ago, a wild storm raged across the Indian Ocean. During the tempest, a ship was smashed to pieces. All the crew drowned, except for one sailor who struggled to a small island.

To his delight, the sailor found that the island was covered in trees laden with fruit. However, when he went to pick some, he discovered that the fruit was actually dazzling gemstones. Exhausted and starving, he fell into a deep sleep.

When he awoke, he found real fruit scattered around him. It had fallen from a large tree growing beside an old well. He ate hungrily, and then stooped over the well to drink. As he stared into the dark water, he saw a vision of the Underworld with its glittering palaces and gardens. At the bottom of the well, a sea-maid was beckoning him.

The sailor leaped into the well and found himself in the Kingdom of Ocean.

"I am the queen of this kingdom," said the sea-maid. "You may be king and share my great wealth, on one condition—you must never touch the statue of the fairy princess, the Apsara."

The sailor promised to do as she asked. Now he lived a most splendid life, but he could not help wondering what would happen if he were to touch the forbidden statue.

One night he crept up to the statue of the Apsara, and gently touched its foot.

Instantly the foot shot out and kicked him with such force that he was catapulted out of the kingdom, up through the well, across the island, and over the sea until he landed with a thud in his own country.

Penniless again, he thought it must all have been a dream—until he found a piece of strange fruit and some seaweed in his pocket.

The Tohunga

In the New Zealand Maori village of Whakatane lived a clever magician, or *tohunga*. The villagers were afraid of the tohunga, so they made a plan to get rid of him.

The men began to prepare for a bird hunt on White Island, a steaming island volcano out in the bay. They loaded their canoes with flax baskets of food and gourds filled with water, for there is no water on that fiery island. Finally they approached the tohunga.

"O great tohunga," they said, "please join our hunting trip so that we may have safe sailing and a good catch."

He agreed to come with them, and they set sail for White Island. The tohunga sat in the place of honor in the stern of the largest canoe.

The hunters reached the island late in the afternoon and caught many seabirds nesting in the sand. After they had prepared the seabird meat for the trip home, they fell asleep in a cave.

Next morning, the tohunga woke up alone, without even a gourd of water. The canoes were already far out on the ocean, heading for home.

The tohunga knew that he had been left on the island to die—but the villagers had forgotten his magic powers.

Taking three flaxbush leaves from his belt, the magician held them high and called on Tangaroa, the great sea spirit, to help him. Immediately, a huge sperm whale broke the surface of the sea. The tohunga swam out and climbed upon its back.

The whale sped toward Whakatane, soon overtaking the canoes. When the hunters finally arrived at the village, they were too ashamed to face the great magician.

The tohunga left Whakatane, never to return. When he died, his spirit entered the ocean and he became a fishtailed *maraki-hau*, or sea god. Now, whenever people are in danger at sea, the maraki-hau comes to their aid. He lifts their heads above water and carries them to safety, just as the whale rescued the tohunga when he was a man of this world.

Soul Cages

An Irishman named Jack Dogherty was strolling along the seashore when he came upon a merman perched on a rock. As it turned out, the merman, or *merrow* as the Irish called mermen, was an old friend of his grandfather's. He invited Jack for dinner, and offered him a magic red feather cap so he could make the underwater journey.

Jack jammed the cap on his head and grabbed hold of the merrow's tail, and down they plunged to the merrow's cottage.

After dinner, the merrow showed Jack his collection of bits and pieces that had dropped into the sea.

"And what do you keep in those?" asked Jack, pointing to some curious wicker cages.

"Oh, those are soul cages," replied the merrow. "When there's a storm above, the souls of drowned fishermen creep inside them to keep warm and dry. Better to be trapped in my cages than roaming about in the cold, wet sea."

As the merrow spoke, Jack heard a muffled sob coming from the nearest cage, and he felt sorry for those poor souls who should have been on their way to heaven. But he said good night to the merrow, who gave him a push up into the sea, and he was home in no time.

The next day, Jack invited the merrow to his own house for a drink or two. He made the merrow's drinks very strong, and soon his guest was fast asleep.

Jack nipped the cap off the merrow's head, raced to the shore, and dived down to the soul cages. One by one he tipped and shook the cages, and then carefully replaced them. As each soul escaped, he saw a tiny flickering flame and heard the sound of a faraway whistle. Then he caught the tail of a large cod and shot out of the sea like a cork out of a bottle.

When Jack returned home, the merman was still asleep. And when he awoke, he was so ashamed of falling asleep that he sneaked off without a word.

Now, whenever sailors are lost at sea, Jack invites the merrow to his house for a drink or two. With the merrow's red cap on his head, he slips away to release the souls from the soul cages.

The merrow never notices that the cages are empty, and to this day, he and Jack are the best of friends.

As old as the oldest Pacific island legend,
as real as the frightened creature caught by Scottish fishermen
   in the nineteenth century,
and as curious as a shriveled, fishtailed fake on show
   in a London coffeehouse,
the mermaid has been many things.

One thing is certain.
Mermaids will continue to splash through our stories
   and swim through our dreams . . .
and one day you might even glimpse one, no matter how strange,
   from the corner of your eye.

Sources

"Yawkyawk Mermaid Dreaming" was recorded and translated from the Rembarrnga Aboriginal language by Adam Saulwick, Maningrida Arts and Culture Centre. The sources of other legends are as follows: "The Merman of Coos Bay" from *Indian Legends of the Pacific North West* by Ella Clark (University of California Press, Berkeley, 1953); "The Sea-Maid and the Apsara" from *Myths of China and Japan* by Donald A. MacKenzie (The Gresham Publishing Co. Ltd., London, 1922); "The Tohunga" from *Fairy Folk Tales of the Maori* by James Cowan (Whitcombe & Tombs, Auckland, 1930); and "Soul Cages" from *Fairy and Folk Tales of Ireland* edited by W. B. Yeats (Macmillan Publishing Co., New York, 1973). The maraki-hau illustrated on pages 6 and 26 are copied from photographs of Whakatane woodcarvings reproduced in James Cowan's *Fairy Folk Tales of the Maori*.

ADDITIONAL INFORMATION CAME FROM THESE SOURCES:

Benwell, G. & Waugh, A. *Sea Enchantress*. Hutchinson, London, 1961.

Blanco, A. & Revah, P. *The Desert Mermaid*. Children's Book Press, San Francisco, 1992.

Briggs, K. *Abbey Lubbers, Banshees & Boggarts: A Who's Who of Fairies*. Kestrel Books, Harmondsworth, England, 1979.

Cherry, J. (ed.). *Mythical Beasts*. British Museum Press, London, 1995.

Coronel, M. *Stories and Legends from Filipino Folklore*. University of Santo Tomas Press, Philippines, 1968.

Dance, P. *Animal Fakes and Frauds*. Sampson Low, Berkshire, England, 1976.

Gachot, T. *Mermaids: Nymphs of the Sea*. Hodder & Stoughton, Sydney, Australia, 1996.

Ritvo, H. *The Platypus and the Mermaid and Other Figments of the Classifying Imagination*. Harvard University Press, Cambridge, Mass., 1997.

The reports of mermaid sightings contained in this book have come from a number of sources, some of them very old. Although they have been recorded as statements of fact, their authenticity cannot be guaranteed.